espresso
education

Story Time

Eddy's Space Adventure

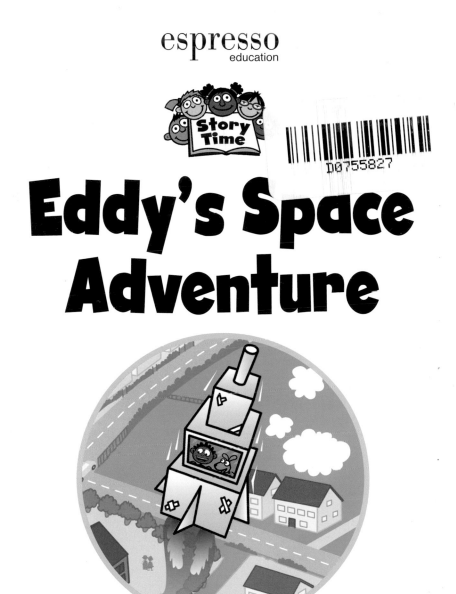

Diane Marwood

W
WATTS

A fantasy story

First published in 2011 by
Franklin Watts
338 Euston Road
London NW1 3BH

Franklin Watts Australia
Level 17/207 Kent Street
Sydney NSW 2000

A CIP catalogue record for this book is
available from the British Library.

ISBN: 978 1 4451 0406 5 (hbk)
ISBN: 978 1 4451 0414 0 (pbk)

Illustrations by Artful Doodlers Ltd.
Art Director: Jonathan Hair
Series Editor: Jackie Hamley
Series Designer: Matthew Lilly

Printed in China

Franklin Watts is a division of
Hachette Children's Books,
an Hachette UK company.
www.hachette.co.uk

Ash, Polly and Eddy were clearing up the shed.

They found some old boxes.
"Let's make a space rocket!"
said Ash.
"Cool!" said Polly. "But you can't
play, Eddy. This is our game."

Polly and Ash stuck the boxes together and covered them with foil. They made a window out of a plastic sheet.

"Now let's show Eddy,"
said Polly. "Eddy!"
she called.

"I can't find Eddy anywhere," said Polly. "Oh no, look!" cried Ash. Polly and Ash's rocket started to shake.

Then, suddenly, the rocket shot high up into the air. Eddy and Scrap were inside!

Eddy and Scrap flew up higher and higher. Down below, they could see the school and the library.

They flew up through the
clouds. The rocket climbed
even higher.

Eddy and Scrap
waved to an
aeroplane...

...whizzed past a satellite...

...and then flew
around the Moon.

They had to hold on tight so they didn't float away!

Suddenly, the rocket started
to speed back down towards
the Earth.

There was the satellite...

...then the
aeroplane.

There was the library
and the school.

At last, the rocket
landed back in
the garden.

Eddy and Scrap tumbled out, laughing. "That was fun!" "Wow!" said Polly. "Can we play too, Eddy?"

Puzzles

Which speech bubbles
belong to Eddy?

Which words describe Eddy
at the start of the story and which
describe him at the end?

annoyed

fed up

excited

cross

happy

thrilled

Answers

Eddy's speech bubbles are: 1, 3, 4

At the start of the story, Eddy is:
annoyed, fed up, cross.
At the end of the story, Eddy is:
excited, happy, thrilled.

Espresso Connections

This book may be used in conjunction with the Literacy area on Espresso
for a speaking and listening and creative writing activity.
Here are some suggestions.

Write your own adventure story

Visit the Story starts section in English 1, and open "Adventure story: A Walk
in Space".

Watch the video together, and ask the children what they think it would be
like to take a walk in space. What would you see? What would you hear?
How would it smell? Would they like to do this?

Ask children to turn to a partner and find out what they think it would be like
in space. Talk about why Eddy and Scrap need to hold on so they don't
float away in this story.

Open the book activity and read the beginning of the book together.

Ask the children to think about what will happen to the rocket man on his
walk in space.

Discuss the possible options – does he float off? How can he get back?

Visit the "Writing resource box" in English 1, and go to the Activity
arcade. Choose the "Writing frame" activity and select "Story – adventure"
on the left. Tab through the information that is given about this genre.

Decide together on the opening of your space adventure story, then on
the problem(s), the events and the ending.

Then perfect your class story in the writing frame, using the word bank on
the left to edit and improve it. Try to use as many space words as you can!